ENCYCLOPEDIA BROWN

and the Case of the Jumping Frogs

Don't miss any of the other books about

ENCYCLOPEDIA BROWN!

ENCYCLOPEDIA BROWN

and the Case of the Jumping Frogs

DONALD J. SOBOL

Illustrated by Robert Papp

DELACORTE PRESS

Published by
Delacorte Press
an imprint of
Random House Children's Books
a division of Random House, Inc.
New York

Visit us on the Web! www.randomhouse.com/kids
Educators and librarians, for a variety of teaching tools, visit us at www.randomhouse.com/teachers

Cataloging-in-Publication data is available from the Library of Congress.
ISBN: 0-385-729316 (trade)   0-385-90148-8 (lib. bdg.)

The text of this book is set in 12-point Goudy.

Printed in the United States of America

October 2003

10 9 8 7 6 5 4 3 2 1

BVG

In memory of a cherished friend
Erik Y. Evren
1926–1999
who went ahead too soon

Contents

The Case of the Rhyming Robber

Police across the nation wondered: How did Idaville do it?

The town had sparkling white beaches, a Little League team, and a computer museum. It had churches, a synagogue, two delicatessens, and four banks. In short, Idaville looked like many other seaside towns.

But it wasn't.

Every person who broke the law in Idaville was caught.

How was this possible?

What was the secret?

Only Mr. and Mrs. Brown knew.

The mastermind behind Idaville's war on crime was their only child. They called him Leroy, and so did his teachers. Everyone else in Idaville called him Encyclopedia.

An encyclopedia is a book or set of books full of facts from A to Z, just like Encyclopedia's head. His friends

1

thought of him as a whole library that could whistle Beethoven.

Mr. Brown was chief of the Idaville police. He was smart and brave. His officers were well trained, honest, and loyal. But sometimes they came up against a crime they could not solve. Then Chief Brown knew where to go—home to dinner.

After saying grace, he went over the case.

Ten-year-old Encyclopedia listened carefully. When he had heard the facts, he asked one question.

One question was all he needed to solve a mystery.

Encyclopedia never spoke about the help he gave his father.

For his part, Chief Brown would have liked to announce to the world, "A bust of my son belongs in the Crimebusters' Hall of Fame."

But who would believe him? Who could believe that the mastermind behind Idaville's spotless police record was a fifth grader?

At dinner Tuesday, Chief Brown toyed with his soup-spoon. Encyclopedia and his mother knew what *that* meant.

The police had come up against a case they couldn't solve.

"Do you want to talk about it, dear?" Mrs. Brown asked gently.

Chief Brown nodded. "A fortune in jewelry belonging to Mrs. Hubert Cushman was stolen from her home last week."

"Give Leroy the facts," Mrs. Brown said. "I'm sure he can help. He's never failed you yet."

Chief Brown laid down his spoon. "The thief who stole Mrs. Cushman's jewelry calls himself The Poet."

"I've heard of him," said Mrs. Brown.

"He steals jewelry and then sends a poem with a riddle in it to his victim," said Chief Brown. "The riddle tells where he buried the jewelry. Mrs. Cushman received her poem yesterday."

"How do his victims know if the riddle really tells where their jewelry is?" Mrs. Brown asked.

"He got careless twice," Chief Brown said. "He made the riddles too easy. The stolen jewelry was found."

"So he really does bury the jewelry," said Mrs. Brown. "What happens when the riddle isn't solved?"

"It's believed that he comes back sometime later, digs up the jewelry, and keeps it."

"My, is he ever something!" exclaimed Mrs. Brown.

"He's what is called a gentleman thief," explained Chief Brown. "Gentlemen thieves commit crimes mainly for the thrill. Outsmarting the police means more than the loot. It's all a sport with them."

Chief Brown took a piece of paper from his breast pocket. He unfolded it and handed it to Mrs. Brown. "This is the riddle Mrs. Cushman received."

Mrs. Brown read it, frowning.

"It doesn't make sense," she said. She passed the sheet

to Encyclopedia. "Here, Leroy. What do you make of it?"

Encyclopedia read The Poet's riddle:

Take the Landsmill Highway north,
And look along the border.
The second clue is marked in reverse,
But the first clue is in order.
The Poet

Encyclopedia had never been on the Landsmill Highway. Nevertheless, he closed his eyes. He always closed his eyes when he did his deepest thinking.

Mr. and Mrs. Brown waited anxiously.

A minute went by, and then another. Had the famous jewel thief, The Poet, outsmarted the boy detective?

Encyclopedia opened his eyes. He asked his one question. "Are there mile markers along the Landsmill Highway, Dad?"

Chief Brown was surprised by the question. "Why, yes, there are."

"Then," said the boy detective, "Mrs. Cushman's jewelry won't be hard to find."

Where was it buried?

(Turn to page 60 for the solution to
The Case of the Rhyming Robber.)

The Case of the Miracle Pill

Encyclopedia helped his father all year round. During the summer he helped the children of the neighborhood as well. He opened his own detective agency in the garage.

Every morning he hung out his sign:

Brown Detective Agency
13 Rover Avenue
Leroy Brown, President
No Case Too Small
25¢ a Day Plus Expenses

To handle the tough kids, he took in a hard-punching fifth grader, Sally Kimball, as his junior partner. Sally was the prettiest girl in the fifth grade. She was also the best athlete.

One morning Encyclopedia and Sally had just opened the Brown Detective Agency for the day when Marsha Murphy stepped in.

"Take a look," she said. "This may be your last chance to see the old me. Soon I'll be in the money."

"Who says?" Sally asked.

"Wilford Wiggins," replied Marsha.

The detectives groaned.

A teenager, Wilford was as lazy as a time-out. Resting was what he did best. Whenever he got to his feet, he tried to fast-talk the little kids of the neighborhood out of their savings.

He never did. Encyclopedia always stopped his shady deals.

"Wilford has called a secret meeting for five o'clock today in the city dump," Marsha said. "He promised to make us little kids so rich we'll be the talk of the continent."

"What's he selling now," Encyclopedia asked, "a breakfast shake made of yeast and car polish for people who want to rise and shine?"

"Wilford's changed," Marsha said. "He told me so himself. He'll never tell another lie."

"Don't worry," Sally said. "You always know when Wilford is lying. His lips move."

Marsha's faith seemed to waver. She laid a quarter on the gas can beside Encyclopedia. "I want to hire you. Maybe Wilford isn't as honest as he says."

"We're hired," Sally said. "See you at the city dump at five o'clock."

When the detectives arrived, Wilford was standing behind a broken table.

On the table were an empty clear plastic bottle, an ice pick, a small jar, a drinking glass, and a pitcher filled with clear liquid.

Wilford started his big sales pitch.

"Gather around," he bellowed at the crowd of little kids waiting for him to fulfill their dreams of untold riches. They edged closer.

"Don't leak a word to any grown-up about the wonder I've got for you," he warned out of the side of his mouth. "They'll take over and cheat you out of every cent."

"Stop beating your gums and get to the big bucks," a boy shouted.

"You're keen for the green, eh, kid?" Wilford purred. "What I have for you today is Antiflow, the world's greatest gift to mankind! The savior of nations, the scientific marvel of the age! Remember the name: *Antiflow!*"

He unscrewed the cap on the plastic bottle and passed the bottle around. Next he took the ice pick and punched a tiny hole in the side of the bottle about an inch from the bottom. Then he filled the bottle from the pitcher. The liquid streamed out of the tiny hole.

Quickly he took a white pill from the jar. He held it up. "Observe: *Antiflow!*"

He dropped the pill into the bottle and screwed on the cap.

Although the bottle was still almost full, liquid stopped streaming out of the hole.

"Baloney!" a girl snapped. "It's a trick. There's something else in there."

"Oh, ye of little faith!" Wilford exclaimed. He filled the water glass from the pitcher and handed it to the girl. "Drink!"

She drank. "It's just water," she said, puzzled.

"Would Wiggins fool you?" Wilford cried. "The secret is the Antiflow. It was invented by Professor Stubblehauser of Germany. He doesn't trust anyone but straight shooters like yours truly. That's why he granted me the rights to sell the miracle pill in the U.S.A. He trusts me to give him half the profits."

Wilford paused to let the moneymaking possibilities of Antiflow sink in.

Then he said, "All my cash is tied up in oil wells. So I'm going to let my little friends in on this chance of a lifetime. For five dollars, you can buy a share in my Antiflow company. The more shares you buy, the more money you'll make!"

"Where's your factory?" a girl demanded.

"I'm glad you asked, friend," Wilford said. "I need your cash to help build the factory. When it's built, I'll make Antiflow by the ton. Don't miss out! Buy shares today at my special low-price, one-day-only offer."

The children talked excitedly among themselves. With Antiflow, floods would be a thing of the past. There were millions in it. Maybe more!

"Buy shares now," Wilford blared. "In a year you can afford to retire your mother and father."

That clinched it. The children lined up, eager to buy shares.

Encyclopedia hurried to the front of the line.

"Put away your money if you don't want a soaking," he said.

How did Encyclopedia know Antiflow was a fake?

(Turn to page 61 for the solution to The Case of the Miracle Pill.)

The Case of the Black Horse

Encyclopedia and Sally were straightening the Browns' garage when Waldo Emerson came in. He looked like he had stepped off a roof, or worse.

"Good to see you, Waldo," Sally said. "We haven't seen you round lately."

"Don't say that word!" Waldo howled.

"Sorry," Sally apologized. "I wasn't thinking."

Waldo had a thing about the word "round." Even when he heard it used harmlessly with other words, as in "round trip" or "round of golf," he threw a fit. It reminded him that some kids still believed the earth was round.

Waldo was the new president of the Idaville Junior Flat Earth Society. He was also the only member.

He laid a quarter on the gasoline can next to Encyclopedia. "I know the detective agency is closed until summer. But I want to hire you."

12

"What for?" Sally asked.

"I wrote an essay for Columbus Day tomorrow," Waldo answered. "The public library is giving a prize for the best essay about the explorer."

"What's the problem?" Encyclopedia asked.

Waldo moaned. "My essay was stolen yesterday. There isn't time to rewrite it. The contest closes at noon today. I wrote about how Columbus proved the earth was flat."

"How did he?" asked Sally.

"He didn't sail off the curve!" Waldo sang.

Encyclopedia never knew when Waldo was serious or having fun.

"I want you to get my essay back," Waldo said. "I'm sure Stinky Redmond stole it. He'll enter my essay as his and win the prize, a book called *The World of Dinosaurs*."

"Have you accused Stinky?" Sally asked.

Waldo rolled his eyes. "Yes, and of course he says he's innocent. He claims *he* wrote the essay. I dared him to meet me in half an hour in South Park at the carousel."

"Carousel," not "merry-go-*round*," Encyclopedia thought instantly. "Why at the carousel, Waldo?"

"The carousel is the scene of the crime," Waldo declared.

"But it doesn't open for an hour," Sally said.

"That's what I want," Waldo replied. "Stinky and I can have it out better with no one there to bother us. If Stinky doesn't show up, I'll know he's guilty."

On the bike ride to the carousel, Sally asked Waldo

what made him believe the earth was flat.

"Most of the earth is made up of water," he said, "and water is flat. Did you ever see a lake or a pond that had a hump in it?"

Sally and Encyclopedia admitted that they had not.

Waldo rolled on.

"The pictures taken of the earth from outer space are fakes," he insisted. "If the earth were a globe, China would be under the United States. My neighbor Mr. Chan comes from China. He would have hung by his feet when he lived there. He didn't. In fact, he has never hung by his feet in all his life."

Waldo reasoned like that.

Stinky Redmond was waiting by the carousel. The double ring of ride-on animals stood silent and still.

Waldo sneered at Stinky. "The thief returns to the scene of his crime! He thought he could get away with stealing my essay!"

"Let's hear what happened," Encyclopedia suggested.

Waldo said, "When I climbed onto the carousel platform yesterday, Stinky was already standing by that black horse."

He pointed to a black horse with one hoof off the ground. It seemed about to prance away. Like all the animals, it had a pole through the back of its neck.

Waldo pointed to a bench beside the black horse. "Before the carousel started, I laid my bag with the essay on that bench," he said. "Stinky swiped it."

"I didn't swipe his bag!" Stinky broke in. "He's afraid my essay will beat his. Mine is oh, so funny. It'll win in a laugh. I wrote that Columbus proved the earth is flat!"

Waldo harrumphed and continued. "Then I got on that white horse," he said, pointing to a white horse three horses in front of the black one. "I never saw you get on the black horse. I never saw you get off. But when the ride ended, I did see you run from the bench like you were legging it for a lifeboat."

"This kid isn't two days out of his tree," Stinky growled. "Sometimes I get sick going up and down, even on a seesaw."

"You weren't on a seesaw," Waldo snapped.

Stinky retorted, "I started getting sick when the black horse moved up and down on the pole as the carousel turned. So I got off and sat on the bench until the ride ended and I felt better. There was a bag on the bench, but I never touched it."

"Why did you rush off the carousel when the ride ended?" Sally asked.

"I had to go to the you-know-where," Stinky mumbled.

Sally whispered to Encyclopedia, "I don't know who to believe. Maybe Waldo never wrote an essay and he's trying to get Stinky in trouble by saying he's a thief. Or maybe it's Stinky who never wrote an essay and stole Waldo's."

"Take another look at the bench and the horses," Encyclopedia suggested.

"I'm looking," Sally said. "Stinky's black horse is three

horses directly behind Waldo's white horse. The bench is just to the left of the black horse."

"Is that all?"

"Yes, except I wish the horses could talk and tell us who is lying."

"One has, in its way," replied the detective.

Who lied, Stinky or Waldo?

**(Turn to page 62 for the solution to
The Case of the Black Horse.)**

The Case of Nemo's Tuba

The detectives were closing the agency for the day when Nemo Huffenwiz, a pudgy sixth grader, blew in. He plunked twenty-five cents on the gas can.

"What's on your mind?" Encyclopedia asked.

"My tuba," Nemo announced. "I know what you're thinking. The tuba is for Tubby Tuba, the fat kid in the back row of the school orchestra."

"Anyone who calls you Tubby Tuba should have his valves ground off," Sally said.

"How may we be of help?" Encyclopedia inquired.

"Find out who played a dirty trick on me and my tuba," said Nemo.

He went over the details of the case for the detectives.

That afternoon the summer youth orchestra had given a performance of Suchalicki's "March of the Frosty Flowers"

in the school auditorium. Nemo was delayed at the dentist's office and arrived at the school late.

Grabbing his tuba from the music room, he had raced to his seat in the rear of the orchestra. Mr. Downing, the conductor, had just raised his baton.

"Boy," said Nemo, "did he give me a look. It curled my shoelaces. Lucky for me I didn't have to play for a while."

"Is it true that in many pieces the tuba doesn't play a single note?" Sally asked.

"Yep," replied Nemo. "In 'March of the Frosty Flowers' the tuba plays only one note. I sweated out forty-two measures before I played it, a high E. If I hit it, I was a hero. If I missed, I was a bum."

Sally cried, "Tell us!"

"I was a bum."

"Oh, dear."

"Someone switched the valves on my tuba," Nemo said. "The valves are what you push down to make the sounds. They should be in order, one, two, three. Someone switched them to three, one, two. You can't tell just by looking if they're in the right order or not. You have to blow."

"Who could have switched them?" Sally asked.

"Anyone," Nemo said. "The instruments belong to the school and are kept in the music room. Kids can practice there or take the instruments home."

"Lugging a tuba home will flatten your feet flatter than a flatiron," Sally warned.

"You're so right," replied Nemo. "That's why the school doesn't allow students to take home the two bass fiddles or the tuba. I practiced the tuba yesterday until the janitor locked the music room for the night."

"Do you suspect anyone?" Sally asked.

"Alma Higgens," Nemo said instantly. "The instruments were handed out in the fall. I got the tuba. Big Alma had wanted it so she could show that a girl is strong enough to carry it. But I was there a minute before her. She had to settle for a trumpet."

"That shouldn't have made her mad enough to pull such a dirty trick on you," Sally said.

"There's more," Nemo said. "This morning I was throwing a baseball with Mitch Jennings on his front lawn. Alma rode by on her bike. I threw wide. The ball whacked her on the foot and she fell off her bike. Oh, boy, was she mad."

"It isn't a good idea to make Alma mad," Sally said. "She's hotheaded."

"The throw was an accident," Nemo said. "But the fall hurt her. Her lip was cut and bleeding a bit, and she was limping. I was sorry and tried to apologize. You should have heard what she said to me!"

"Alma could have sneaked into school before the performance of 'March of the Frosty Flowers' and switched the valves on your tuba," Sally said. "Limping or not."

"I believe it's time to question Alma," Encyclopedia said.

On the way to Alma's house, he stopped at the school to speak with Mr. Downing, the conductor.

When Encyclopedia came out, he said, "Mr. Downing told me Alma telephoned him before the concert. She said she hurt herself falling off her bike this morning. She was staying home to rest and practice the trumpet."

At Alma's house, Sally rang the doorbell. Alma opened the door.

"What's the squawk?" she demanded, glaring at Nemo.

"I just remembered," Nemo whispered to Encyclopedia. "I don't want to be here."

Sally stepped fearlessly up to the big girl. "We think you switched the valves on Nemo's tuba. You wanted him to miss his one big note, a high E."

"So Mr. Downing would think I wasn't good enough and kick me out of the orchestra," Nemo put in, his courage up. "Then you'd take over the tuba."

"Think again, mousehead," Alma snarled. "I wasn't near the school today."

"Where were you?" Sally demanded.

"After I telephoned Mr. Downing to tell him I couldn't make it today because I hurt my foot, I went to my room. I read and practiced the trumpet."

"How come we didn't hear you playing?" Sally demanded.

"I quit practicing a few minutes ago," Alma said. "Besides, I use a mute. I can barely be heard in the next room. I'm the kind who respects the ears of others. Now bye-bye, you sand fleas."

She shut the front door with a bang.

"I sure hope she's guilty," declared Nemo. "If she isn't, she's going to make me pay for saying she is. Maybe I ought to give her the tuba and take up barrel jumping."

"Don't," Encyclopedia said. "Alma switched the valves."

How did Encyclopedia know?

**(Turn to page 63 for the solution to
The Case of Nemo's Tuba.)**

The Case of the Ring in the Reef

Hector Heywood was nearly in tears when he came into the Brown Detective Agency.

"Bugs Meany, that no-good bully!" he wailed.

"Oh, not Bugs again!" exclaimed Sally.

Bugs was the leader of a gang of tough older boys. When Encyclopedia and Sally weren't around, they bullied the little kids of the neighborhood.

The boys called themselves the Tigers, but they should have called themselves the Spurs. They always arrived on the heels of trouble.

Sally often said Bugs was quite accomplished for a boy with the IQ of a refrigerator door.

"What's Bugs done now?" Encyclopedia asked Hector.

"He stole Mrs. van Colling's diamond ring from me," Hector replied.

He explained. He had been at the beach the day before. He'd found a ring in the sand. The ring hadn't looked valuable, but he had taken it home.

"This morning the *Idaville Gazette* had a story about the ring," Hector said. "It's worth a lot of money, and there's a reward for finding it. The newspaper said the ring belonged to Mrs. van Colling."

"I read the story," Encyclopedia said. "Mrs. van Colling thought she had lost it while scuba diving at Warren Reef. She hired two divers to search for the ring. They didn't find it."

"That's because she lost it on the beach," Hector said. "I was returning the ring when Bugs and three of his Tigers stopped me a block from her house. They asked where I was going, and like a dummy I told them. They turned me upside down. They shook me until the ring fell out of my pocket."

Hector laid a quarter on the gas can. "Get the ring back. I found it. I should get the reward, not Bugs."

Encyclopedia agreed. "We'll go see Bugs."

"You go," said Hector. "I'm about to do what any red-blooded coward would do—go home. Bugs is too rough for kids our age."

"Except one," Encyclopedia said. "Sally has straightened him out before."

It was true. The last time Sally and Bugs had fought, the toughest Tiger had taken a right to the nose. His eyes had

rolled up far enough to see his brains. For a full minute he had staggered around as if looking for the rest of himself.

"Okay, I'll go with you to see Bugs," Hector said. "But you'd better have an escape plan."

The Tigers' clubhouse was an unused toolshed behind Sweeney's auto body shop. Bugs was sitting on a crate out front.

He had a deck of cards and was practicing dealing himself all the aces.

When he spied the detectives and Hector, he growled, "Well, well, the little goody-goods." His lips curved in a sneer. "Go adopt an egg!"

"Don't get your dandruff up, Bugs," Sally said. "Hector told us he found Mrs. van Colling's ring on the beach yesterday. He says you took it from him."

"What is this?" Bugs growled. "You dare accuse Bugs Meany, the idol of America's youth, of being a common thief? I found the ring! I'm waiting until I think Mrs. van Colling has had her breakfast before I return it. I'm a gentleman."

He took a step toward Hector, his teeth bared.

"I don't think he wants to be friends," Hector whispered to Encyclopedia. "I have what I believe is a very good idea: Run for your life!"

Encyclopedia grabbed his arm and held him.

"Stay calm," the detective said. "Trust Sally."

"Where did you find the ring, Bugs?" Sally demanded.

27

"I often dive at dawn," Bugs purred. "The reef is so beautiful then! The pursuit of beauty is my life. I don't get along on good looks alone."

"Where did you find the ring?" Sally repeated.

"If you must know, I was swimming by the reef when my foot struck something lying on the bottom," Bugs said. "It was a bright yellow fish, dead. I moved it with my foot. I saw what had been lying under it. A ring!"

"Aw, c'mon, Bugs," Sally said. "That's the biggest fish story I ever heard."

"You doubt the word of Bugs Meany?" Bugs said, his voice rising. "Nobody gets away with calling me a liar!"

He took aim and threw his Sunday punch. Sally sidestepped and cracked him one on the side of the jaw. *Zowie!*

Bugs spun like a propeller. Encyclopedia thought he saw Bugs's face and the back of his head at the same time.

Bugs slowed, wobbled, and fell flat. He lifted his head and moaned, "I hate it when she does that."

Sally suddenly looked concerned. "Oh, no. Maybe he's telling the truth!"

"He isn't," Encyclopedia said.

What made Encyclopedia so sure?

(Turn to page 64 for the solution to The Case of the Ring in the Reef.)

The Case of the Lawn Mower Races

Encyclopedia and Sally arrived at the county lawn mower racing championships at five minutes to nine on Saturday morning.

Engines roared. Billows of dust and smoke rose from the track, a nine-acre pasture on Josh Woodly's farm. Rows of spotlights and bales of hay outlined the course.

Souped-up, bladeless riding mowers bounced over ruts and bumps at speeds of more than forty miles an hour. The riders were finishing the last few laps of the twelve-hour endurance race, which had begun at nine o'clock the night before.

Three of the detectives' classmates—Larry Winslow, Bill Marshall, and Ken Uster—were in the crowd.

"You got here just in time," Larry said to the detectives. "This race ends in a few minutes."

Encyclopedia watched the seven mowers scream around the curves.

"How come there are only seven mowers in this race?" Sally asked.

Ken explained. Twenty mowers had started, each driven by a team of two men and a woman. Fifteen teams had to retire. Most of them had gone to the hospital with headaches, sprains, cuts, and bruises.

"Racing lawn mowers can be hard on your health," Bill observed.

The crowd began cheering. A teenager, Mary Mullins, had taken the lead. She crossed the finish line the winner.

Her two teammates rushed to congratulate her. Autograph hunters held out pen and pencil. She looked very tired, but she signed everything put in front of her.

"The next race is a one-miler," Larry said. "The rules are different from the twelve-hour race. No pit stops for fuel are allowed. The engine has to be the one that came with the mower. So the mowers can't go as fast as in the twelve-hour race."

"What you *can* do," added Bill, "is change the driving gears or pulleys to send more power to the wheels. That gives you more speed."

The contestants in the one-mile race were announced. Larry's twin brother, Bill's aunt, and Ken's cousin were all competing. Mary Mullins was in the race, too. The

detectives and a few of the crowd, including Bill, Ken, and Larry, followed Mary to her trailer in the parking lot. On the trailer was her shiny new mower. It had yellow racing stripes and countless coats of polish.

She tightened the wide belt that held her insides in place going over the bumps. After adjusting her crash helmet, she pushed the mower to the starting line.

The command came. "Ladies and gentlemen, start your engines!"

All ten mowers sputtered to life.

The drivers leaped aboard. They quickly attached a cut-off switch to their bodysuits. If a driver was thrown off the mower, the engine stopped.

The starting gun sounded. The mowers roared down the course.

Mary Mullins didn't get far. She hit two bumps and her mower died.

Jumping to the ground, she peered at the engine. Ken, Larry, Bill, and the detectives rushed over to help.

"The nut and bolt that hold the line from the gas tank to the carburetor fell off," she said. "Luckily, the line hung upright or gas would have spilled all over the course. I just lost the gas in the carburetor."

She shook her head, puzzled. "Everything was tight yesterday. The engine ran beautifully."

She glanced at the mowers racing away. "If I find the

nut and bolt and can get wrenches quickly, I can at least finish."

"I'll get the wrenches," Bill volunteered. "Where do you keep them?"

"All my socket wrenches and open-end wrenches are in the toolbox in my truck," Mary said.

"I'm on my way," Bill said.

While he was gone, Ken, Larry, and the detectives helped Mary search for the nut and bolt.

"Here's a nut!" Ken cried. He picked it up from the grass a few yards past the first bump. Larry found a bolt past the second bump.

Mary said the nut and bolt were hers.

Bill came running back. "I brought an open-end wrench *and* a socket wrench just to be safe."

Using the wrenches, Mary tightened the bolt and nut in place. She started the engine and set off in hot pursuit of the other mowers.

"The nut and bolt were loosened by someone who didn't want Mary Mullins to win the one-mile race," Sally mused. "It was easy to do while everyone was watching the finish of the twelve-hour race."

"That makes sense," Encyclopedia murmured.

Sally frowned. "The guilty person wanted someone besides Mary to win. That makes Larry, Bill, and Ken suspects. They each had a family member in the race. Or it could have been someone else. *Anyone!*"

"No, not just anyone," corrected Encyclopedia.

"Don't tell me you know who did it," Sally said.

Encyclopedia nodded. "I do."

Do you?

(Turn to page 65 for the solution to The Case of the Lawn Mower Races.)

The Case of the Jumping Frogs

Buddy Mayfair, better known as Ribbet, was the only fifth grader anyone knew who ran a college for frogs.

"It's frog-catching season," he announced, hopping into the Brown Detective Agency.

During frog-hunting season, Ribbet warmed up by hopping a lot.

"The science club is hunting frogs at South Park at two o'clock today," he said. "Stinky Redmond and Alma Higgens aren't coming. Want to take their places?"

Encyclopedia and Sally didn't have to be asked twice. They had never been on a frog hunt.

"I'm glad Stinky and Alma aren't coming," Sally said. "They're always a problem."

A high steel fence surrounded the campgrounds at

South Park. Standing by one of the two gates was a park ranger. Beside him were the other campers and Mr. Sands, the science teacher. Mr. Sands was in charge of the outing.

He welcomed the detectives, who were the last children to arrive. "We'll be the only group in the campgrounds today. Come inside."

The ranger locked the gate behind them. He climbed into a small pickup truck and drove off.

"There are two gates, and both are locked when everyone is inside the campgrounds," Ribbet said. "It's for the campers' safety. Mr. Sands has a key—"

He broke off. A rumbling had grown into a full roar. A huge tractor was coming straight toward the gate.

The driver unlocked the gate, drove in, and then locked the gate behind him.

"I'm cutting a firebreak," he told the children. "Sorry about the noise the disks make."

Behind the tractor was a row of twelve steel cutting disks. At both ends of the row were wheels with thick tires. The wheels could be lowered, thus lifting the disks off the ground when not in use.

With a friendly wave to the children, he slowly drove on. The disks churned roots, shrubs, and stumps, leaving a fireproof trail.

Unlocking the far gate, he drove through and locked it again.

"Frogs are waiting," Mr. Sands called when the campers had pitched their tents and spread their bedrolls. "Let's head to the pond."

The boys and girls hurried through the gate, which Mr. Sands locked behind them.

"You can't be too careful," Ribbet said. "Lots of things have been stolen from the park lately."

The pond lay beyond a woods out of sight of the campgrounds. During the walk, Ribbet fine-tuned himself with hops every few steps.

"I hope the hunting is good," he said. "I need a big enrollment."

For the past two years Ribbet had trained frogs for others at his frog college. His students always did well at frog-jumping contests.

Not only did Ribbet teach his student frogs quick takeoffs and how to race. They got a room and all the flies they could eat.

Other services included massages and calisthenic drills, plus time off to swim in the family birdbath.

All for fifteen cents a day.

"I started the college two years ago after my bullfrog, General Grant, set a state record," Ribbet said. "The General covered seventeen feet two inches in the three jumps. I retired him. He's now my poster boy."

"How's business this year?" Encyclopedia inquired.

"Only fair," Ribbet answered. "Right now I'm training frogs for two grown-ups and three kids."

The day's hunting didn't go well. Although the *ribbet, ribbet* of frogs filled the air, the only creatures found were tadpoles.

"We'll do better tonight," Encyclopedia said.

Back at the campgrounds the children perked up by playing among the tracks in the firebreak. Led by Ribbet, they leapfrogged from one tire track to another. He was having so much fun he ran to get his camera from his tent.

The fun ended when Ribbet discovered that his camera had been stolen.

"I should have taken it with me to the pond," he groaned. "But I was afraid of dropping it in the drink."

"The thief can't be one of us," Sally insisted. "The whole group went to the pond together and came back together."

Mr. Sands was upset by the theft. He fetched the ranger.

The ranger examined the locks on both gates. They were unbroken.

"Only you and me and Hal, the tractor driver, have a key to the gates," the ranger said to Mr. Sands. "Hal said he never returned to the campgrounds after cutting the firebreak. I stayed in my office after I left you."

The ranger chuckled. "I don't think it was a thief at all," he said. "Probably it was a caterpillar. Everyone knows what shutterbugs they are. The camera will turn up."

"Only a fool of a thief would risk climbing over the fence," Mr. Sands mused.

"The thief didn't have to," said Encyclopedia.

Mr. Sands stared at Encyclopedia, startled. "Do you know who stole the camera?"

"Why, yes," said the detective, "though he had me stumped for a time."

Who was the thief?

(Turn to page 66 for the solution to The Case of the Jumping Frogs.)

The Case of the Toy Locomotive

On Wednesday Encyclopedia and Sally went with Sol Calvin to the Best Buy Toy Company factory for the yearly auction. Sol's sister Birdie worked there.

She tested toys, though she didn't know it.

Birdie was four years old.

The toy factory was in a large red brick building. Sol led the detectives to a room in which there were five small children aged three to four, two teachers, and lots of toys. One of the teachers was reading a book of fairy tales to the children.

"Golly," Sally said. "It looks like a classroom in a nursery school."

"It is," Sol said. "The little kids report for classes here three days a week. They listen to stories, finger paint, dress up in costumes, and eat snacks. The most important period

41

is free time. That's when they play with the toys the company makes."

"What toys are being sold today at the auction?" Sally asked.

"Toys the kids are tired of," Sol replied, "or toys that have flopped. If the kids don't like a new toy, it doesn't get into stores."

"Is that good business?" objected Sally. "I mean, five little kids forcing their tastes on the whole country."

"The Best Buy Toy Company doesn't let that happen," Sol answered. "The testers change. A new group of little kids enrolls every two weeks."

He pointed to a large mirror.

"It's a one-way mirror," he said. "Company officers sit behind the mirror. They can see the kids but the kids can't see them."

"The kids have no idea they're testing the toys?" Sally said.

"Correct," Sol said. "The officers and the teachers make careful notes about which new toys are liked or disliked."

"That's neat," said Encyclopedia. "The kids don't have to give answers they feel the company wants to hear."

The teacher who had been reading to the class closed the book. "Free play time," she announced.

The young toy-testers immediately went to work. Some chose toys and played quietly and happily.

Others weren't happy. They had chosen one or another

of the newer toys. When it failed to please, it was shaken, sat on, or cast aside.

Sol's sister Birdie was busily banging a red car on the floor. A wheel flew off.

Birdie wailed.

"That car will go back to the drawing board," Sol said.

The auction was going to start soon. The small toys were displayed on a long table. Bigger toys were on the floor. An electric locomotive caught Encyclopedia's eye.

"Do kids this little really play with electric trains?" he asked.

"Hardly," Sol said. "The locomotive belongs to one of the men in bookkeeping. It's pretty beat up, but he hopes it will sell. I want it. If the bidding goes past five dollars and twenty cents, though, I'm sunk. Five dollars and twenty cents is all I have."

The nursery was filling up with parents. Just before the bidding began, Sledge O'Hara, Bugs Meany's eleven-year-old cousin, came in.

Sledge's right arm was in a sling. He had hurt his shoulder badly in a card game trying to catch a joker. It had fallen out of his sleeve.

The auction began. The prices were a bargain hunter's dream. Everyone was having fun except Sol.

His bid for the locomotive fell eighty cents short. Sledge bought it for six dollars.

"What happens if the locomotive doesn't work?" Sledge

demanded of Mr. Wilmott, the auctioneer and a vice president of the Best Buy Toy Company.

"Return it, and the company will let you pick another toy free of charge," said Mr. Wilmott. He put the locomotive in a gift bag.

Sledge slipped his left arm through the handles and slung the bag over his left shoulder. He strutted from the nursery, grinning slyly.

Ten minutes later he was back, empty-handed.

"Two big teenagers stole my locomotive!" he howled.

He had left by the revolving door in the rear of the factory, he said. A big teenager got in the slot ahead of him and dropped a package. It jammed the door.

"I was stuck, trapped like a rat!" Sledge cried.

Another big teenager, he went on, snatched the bag with the locomotive. Both thieves got clean away.

"I was robbed in your building," Sledge said to Mr. Wilmott. "You're responsible. You owe me for my pain and suffering. But I'm not pushy. I'll take another toy."

"Sledge is such a liar and a cheat," Sol muttered. "I'd go over Niagara Falls on a banana peel before I'd believe him."

"Did anyone see the thieves?" Mr. Wilmott asked calmly.

"No, the theft is just another chapter in my life of toil and hardship," Sledge moaned.

"Why did you leave by the back door?" Mr. Wilmott inquired.

"Because my bus home stops behind the building," Sledge answered. "The streets are so unsafe these days, I wanted to get to the bus as quickly as possible. An honest lad like me doesn't stand a chance alone. We're in a crime wave! Bad guys are everywhere!"

Mr. Wilmott hesitated, and then said, "Well . . . all right. Pick another toy."

Sledge grinned and tapped a music box. "This will do," he sang.

"Encyclopedia!" Sally exclaimed. "Sledge will walk off with both the locomotive and the music box for six dollars! You can prove he wasn't robbed, can't you?"

The detective smiled his knowing smile. "Of course."

What was the proof?

(Turn to page 67 for the solution to The Case of the Toy Locomotive.)

The Case of the Air Guitar

Encyclopedia and Sally were biking in town when they saw Scott Burlow in an alley. Scott was dancing like a chicken on a hot stove.

The fingers of his left hand, which were next to his shoulder, slid up and down, twitching like crazy. His right hand seemed to be scratching his hip, and he was shaking his head so fast that it looked like it might snap right off his neck.

"Oh, dear," said Sally. "I hope he doesn't get whiplash."

"Maybe he just ate his first raw oyster," Encyclopedia offered hopefully.

Scott saw the detectives and stopped dancing and twitching and scratching and shaking.

"Scott! What itches?" Sally inquired anxiously.

Scott laughed. "Nothing. I'm tuning up is all. Today is the day."

"For what?" Encyclopedia was almost afraid to ask.

"You're detectives," Scott said. "I'll give you a clue. Check out my hair."

"It's long," Sally said.

"I grew it an extra five inches for the air guitar contest," Scott said. "You have to look like a musician if you want to catch the eye of the judges."

Encyclopedia had heard of air guitar contests, in which the performers pretended to play a guitar. The guitar couldn't be seen or heard because it didn't exist.

"I finished third last year," Scott said. "I'm not resting on my laurels. A win today and I'm in the state finals."

Sally said, "We were on our way to the early movie. But we'd rather see you play air guitar."

"Come on. The contest starts at eleven-thirty at the dance school on Third Street," Scott said.

The detectives went with Scott to the dance school. The main room had some two dozen folding chairs in front of a stage.

The stage was empty except for a piano.

"I'll show you around," Scott said.

He led the detectives backstage, where the equipment was stored.

He pointed toward a door. "That leads to the office."

"There's someone in there," Sally whispered. "Listen."

Two boys were speaking in low voices.

"Make sure it's his and not one of ours."

"It's his. Let's go. It's nearly twenty minutes past eleven."

"You're fast. It's only eleven-eighteen—oops, eleven-nineteen."

"Who's in there?" Scott called.

Encyclopedia opened the door as the other door in the office slammed shut. He crossed the office and opened the other door. It led to the street.

"We're too late," Encyclopedia said.

Whoever had been in the office had turned the corner and was out of sight.

"I don't like this," Scott muttered.

They went back into the main room and took seats. Friends and relatives of the air guitar players were filing in.

Mrs. Watson, the elementary school music teacher, sat down at the piano. She placed several sets of sheet music on the rack above the keyboard.

"Each person performs to the music he's chosen," Scott explained.

At eleven-thirty, Mr. Jurgens, one of the two judges, announced the six contestants.

Scott and the other five performers took off their wristwatches and laid them on the piano.

"Each kid has exactly one minute to perform," Scott explained upon returning to his seat beside the detectives. "You lose points if you stop playing more than ten seconds before or after the music ends."

"So no one can cheat by checking his watch?" said Sally.

"That's the idea," Scott said. "The judges look for artistic style, ability to stay with the music, and airiness."

First up was Adam Lang. He wore a red wig and played his invisible guitar to "Rowdy Rob Robin."

He flung himself this way and that. Alas, he became dizzy, lost his footing, and knocked himself out in twenty-two seconds.

Scott, Harold Johnson, Phil Twining, and Manny Foster had their turns. Each strummed the air wildly, hopping and flopping as though hooked to a live wire.

"It's going to be a tough call," Scott remarked. "We all cracked down without cracking up."

Herb Carter was last to perform. "Herb won last year," Scott said. "He really rattles his bones. He's going to be hard to beat."

Herb swaggered onto the stage, grinning confidently. He spread his feet, ready to do his thing the moment Mrs. Watson started playing.

She didn't play. She fumbled through the stack of music she had on the piano.

"I can't find Herb's piece!" she exclaimed. "I'm sure I had it in the office with the other music for safekeeping."

"Those two boys who were talking in the office stole Herb's music!" Sally whispered. "It has to be! But which two?"

"Couldn't you tell by their voices who the thieves are, Scott?" Encyclopedia asked.

Scott shook his head. "They were speaking too quietly,"

he answered. "Without his own music, Herb doesn't stand a chance."

Herb performed bravely, but clearly not well enough to win.

The judges counted up the scores.

Encyclopedia used the break to stroll onto the stage and over to the piano. Sally followed him.

The boy detective studied the watches.

Five of the watches had a minute hand and an hour hand. The sixth watch had no hands—it showed the time digitally.

"*Hmm*," Encyclopedia said.

"What does '*hmm*' mean?" Sally demanded.

"It means I know who one of the thieves is," Encyclopedia answered. "From him, we'll learn the name of the other."

What was the clue?

(Turn to page 68 for the solution to The Case of the Air Guitar.)

The Case of the Backwards Runner

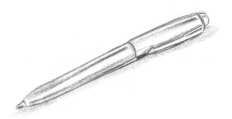

Encyclopedia and Sally were biking by the Grove Shopping Center when they saw a fight about to break out.

Felix McGee and Rupert Dugan were on the sidewalk near the exit lane of the parking lot, screaming in each other's faces.

Oscar, a security guard, was trying to keep them from putting their fists in each other's faces.

It wasn't easy. Both boys were built like barrels.

Felix played tackle on the seventh-grade football team. Rupert was the star of the seventh-grade wrestling team.

"Those two have never liked each other," Sally said. "In fact, they hate each other."

"We'd better find out what this is about," Encyclopedia said.

The detectives walked their bikes onto the sidewalk.

Felix shook his fist under Rupert's nose. "You're cleared for takeoff, fatso!"

Rupert shook his fist under Felix's jaw. "If I hit you with this, you'd better have wings that fit you."

Oscar was glad to see Encyclopedia and Sally. He wouldn't have to separate the two boys by force. He let the young detectives take over.

Felix and Rupert were glad, too. They were saved from having to make good their threats to punch each other out.

Oscar told the detectives what had happened. A few minutes earlier, he had seen a boy palm a silver pen from a counter in Fabian's Gift Shoppe. The boy shoved it into his pocket and legged it out of there.

"I chased him outside," Oscar said. "He ran from the parking lot down the exit lane to the street."

"You never saw the thief's face?" Sally asked.

"No, I saw only his back," Oscar said. "I lost sight of him for a moment when a pickup truck drove between us. Then I saw these two boys. Both were dressed like the thief, in a white T-shirt, blue shorts, and sneakers. They were quarreling. Neither had the pen on him."

"That's because I saw Felix toss something small into a pickup truck that was driving past," Rupert said. "It must have been the pen he stole."

"He could have," Oscar admitted. "I didn't see that because the pickup truck passed between us."

"Felix had to get rid of it before you caught up with

him," Rupert continued. "It was evidence. Now it's out. He's been living a dark and secret life—the life of a shoplifter!"

"I didn't steal anything. I didn't toss anything into a truck," Felix insisted. "Rupert did."

"Then why were you running?" Encyclopedia asked.

"Because I had to be home by noon for my aunt's birthday party. I ran because I realized it was noon and I was late."

"Without a watch, how did you know it was noon?" Sally said, pointing to Felix's bare wrist.

"I was in the bookstore when I heard the bells in the church behind the shopping center. They chime at noon," Felix replied.

Oscar nodded. "The church bells did chime."

Felix said, "My house is only three blocks away. I figured if I ran like crazy I wouldn't be more than a couple of minutes late. Now I'll really be late."

Encyclopedia turned to Rupert. "What were you doing near the shopping center?"

"I was jogging," he answered. "I like to keep in shape."

"The shape of a watermelon," Felix said.

"I had jogged past the exit lane when I saw Felix running down it," Rupert said. "I saw him toss something small and shiny into a passing truck. It must have been the pen. I stopped to see what was going on."

"How could you see Felix running down the exit lane?" demanded Sally. "You just said you had jogged *past* it. That means you had your back to him."

"I was jogging backwards when I saw Felix running," Rupert said. "I always jog backwards when the sun is in my eyes, like today. Everything that forwards running messes up, backwards running puts right. Backwards running helps the knees and hips and is easier on the joints. But it's tiring."

"You hunk of blubber!" Felix cried. "You didn't see anything."

"I know what I saw," Rupert said. "You didn't want Oscar to find the pen on you, so you threw it into a passing truck. My eyes don't lie."

"Oh, yeah?" Felix snapped. "You remind me of an ostrich. An ostrich's eye is bigger than its brain."

"Oh, yeah?" Rupert retorted. "You remind me of a starfish. A starfish *has* no brain."

"Encyclopedia," Sally whispered. "What do you think? Felix could have stolen the pen and tossed it into the truck before Oscar caught up with him. Or Rupert could have stolen the pen and dumped it in the truck himself."

"A case about a pen is a case about words," answered the detective. "Therefore, the boy who didn't tell the truth is—"

Who didn't tell the truth, Rupert or Felix?

(Turn to page 69 for the solution to The Case of the Backwards Runner.)

Solutions

The Case of the Rhyming Robber

When Chief Brown said there were mile markers along the border of the Landsmill Highway, Encyclopedia knew where the jewelry was buried.

The last two lines of the riddle told him.

The line "But the first clue is in order" meant that the first number of the mile marker was forty. It is the only number in the English language whose letters are in alphabetical order.

The second number of the mile marker was one. It is the only number in English whose letters are in reverse alphabetical order.

Therefore, Mrs. Cushman's jewelry was buried by or under marker forty-one.

Chief Brown ordered a stakeout of mile marker forty-one. Six days later, The Poet was captured as he dug up Mrs. Cushman's jewelry.

The Case of the Miracle Pill

Encyclopedia realized what was stopping the water from coming out of the small hole near the bottom of the bottle.

It was not the Antiflow pill, which was nothing but a piece of wood painted white.

It was the bottle cap.

Had Wilford not screwed the cap on tightly, the water would have continued to come out of the hole.

Prove this for yourself. Do as Wilford did. Let water flow out a small hole near the bottom of a plastic bottle.

Now press the palm of your hand over the top of the bottle or screw the cap on tightly.

The water will stop coming out until you remove your hand or loosen the cap!

Wilford was forced to admit the pill was a fake and stopped trying to sell Antiflow.

The Case of the Black Horse

Stinky said he had become sick when his horse moved up and down on its pole. He had gone to the bench to recover.

He had already seen Waldo carrying the bag toward the carousel. He had stood by the black horse as if preparing to mount. The black horse was three horses behind Waldo's white one. Hence, once the carousel began to turn, Waldo was unlikely to look back and see what Stinky was up to.

Stinky never sat on the black horse.

When the ride started, he went straight to the bench to see what was in the bag. He was too busy reading Waldo's essay to notice his mistake.

But Encyclopedia noticed.

A carousel horse with three feet (or four feet) on the ground, like the black horse, doesn't move up and down. It doesn't move at all! Stinky couldn't have gotten sick!

Stinky returned Waldo's essay. It won second prize, a globe.

The Case of Nemo's Tuba

Alma wanted to get even with Nemo for beating her to the tuba and knocking her off her bike. So she telephoned Mr. Downing, the orchestra conductor. She told him that she was hurt and couldn't get to school to play in "March of the Frosty Flowers." She promised to practice the trumpet at home.

Alma thought that gave her an alibi. How could she have switched the valves on the tuba if she wasn't at the school?

Encyclopedia knew better.

She had hurt not only her foot, but her lip, too. It was bleeding when she fell off the bike.

She couldn't have been at home blowing a trumpet with a cut lip.

Caught in the lie, she confessed. She had switched the valves on Nemo's tuba.

Mr. Downing moved her from the trumpet to the triangle.

Nemo kept the tuba.

The Case of the
Ring in the Reef

Bugs had also read about the lost ring in the *Idaville Gazette*. He had to say he found the ring in the water around the reef where Mrs. van Colling thought she had lost it.

That would prove how smart he was, smarter than the divers she had hired.

The divers would have searched all the parts of the reef. But they wouldn't have bothered to look under a dead yellow fish lying on the bottom. At least that's what Bugs thought.

He was right. The divers didn't look under the fish because it wasn't there.

Fish that haven't been dead long enough to lose their color don't sink to the bottom. They float near the surface.

Caught like a fish out of water, Bugs admitted taking the ring from Hector. Truth, he decided, hurt less than Sally's fists. He gave back the ring.

Hector received the reward, a wristwatch that told time underwater.

The Case of the Lawn Mower Races

Having just finished the twelve-hour race, Mary Mullins was very tired. So she accepted Bill Marshall's offer to go and get wrenches rather than get them herself.

Bill offered to get the wrenches to throw suspicion off himself by helping Mary.

He didn't fool Encyclopedia.

Being tired, Mary Mullins forgot to tell Bill the size of the wrenches she needed. But he fetched the right size wrenches for the nut and bolt!

Bill could not have known what size wrenches to bring unless he was the one who had *loosened* the nut and bolt.

Mary finished last in the one-miler.

But she had helped her teammates win the twelve-hour race. Their prize was a free trip to Washington, D.C., and the honor of mowing the south lawn of the White House.

Bill was banned from the mower races for five years.

SOLUTION TO

The Case of the Jumping Frogs

The thief was Hal, the tractor driver.

He had cut a firebreak, leaving a trail of ground-up bushes, rocks, and stumps. Then he had come back and stolen Ribbet's camera while everyone was frog hunting.

Hal had told the ranger he hadn't driven the tractor into the campgrounds again.

Encyclopedia proved he had.

After the frog hunt, the children had returned to the campgrounds and played leapfrog among the *tire tracks* in the firebreak.

Encyclopedia reasoned that the driver had lowered the wheels and raised the disks in order to travel quietly. The tire tracks showed he had driven into the campgrounds *after* cutting the firebreak.

Thanks to Encyclopedia's sharp brain, Ribbet got his camera back. Hal was fired.

The Case of the Toy Locomotive

Encyclopedia saw through Sledge's lie.

A revolving door turns counterclockwise. So Sledge would have had his right arm to the open side of his door.

But Sledge had his right arm in a sling. The bag was over his left shoulder.

No thief would risk taking the time to squeeze into the revolving door with Sledge, reach around him, pull down his left arm, which was pushing the door, yank the bag free, and squeeze out again. Thieves would target someone carrying a bag over their right (or outside) shoulder.

Sledge confessed. The locomotive had not been stolen. He had hidden it, intending to come back for it. He had made up the theft so he could get another toy free.

Sledge kept the locomotive, which he had paid for, but gave back the music box. Sol bought the music box for five dollars and twenty cents and gave it to Birdie.

SOLUTION TO
The Case of the
Air Guitar

One of the two boys overheard in the office said, "It's nearly twenty minutes past eleven." That's the way someone looking at a watch with hands states the time.

The other boy answered, "You're fast. It's only eleven-eighteen." That's the way someone with a watch that shows numbers digitally states the time. Then he added, "Oops, eleven-nineteen." That meant a number (the minute number, in this case) had changed, as numbers do on a digital watch.

The digital watch belonged to Phil Twining. He confessed. He and Manny Foster had dumped Herb's music down the sewer, hoping to better their chance of winning.

The judges disqualified them. They let Herb select another piece of music. He chose Scott's piece, "The Tasmanian Jump."

As he hadn't practiced to "The Tasmanian Jump," Herb finished second, behind Scott, who won.

The Case of the Backwards Runner

In his eagerness to frame Felix as the thief, Rupert made a slip of the tongue. He said he saw Felix running down the exit lane after he had jogged *past* it.

That meant his back was to Felix. Sally caught the mistake.

So Rupert had to come up with an explanation fast. He said he was jogging backwards, and that was how he could see Felix.

"I always jog backwards when the sun is in my eyes, like today," he said.

That was his second mistake.

Encyclopedia knew the sun couldn't have been in Rupert's eyes, whether he had been jogging forwards or backwards.

It was noon, as the church bells proclaimed. Hence, the sun was directly overhead.

Rupert's father made him pay for the pen. The coach of the wrestling team made him run one mile after practice each day *backwards*.

About the Author

Donald J. Sobol is the award-winning author of more than sixty-five books for young readers. He lives in Florida with his wife, Rose, who is also an author. They have three grown children. The Encyclopedia Brown books have been translated into fourteen languages.